Went up
the water spout.

Down came
the rain,

The Itsy-Bitsy Spider

Rosemary Wells

Scholastic Press ♦ New York

The itsy-bitsy spider

Bunny Reads Back 

The Itsy-Bitsy Spider

Rosemary Wells

Bunny Reads Back

Reading together twenty minutes a day is the most important gift you can give your child. Read to your bunny often, and your bunny will read back to you. — ROSEMARY WELLS

And washed
the spider out.

Out came
the sun,

And dried up
all the rain.

And the
itsy-bitsy spider
went up the spout
again.

Again!

Published by Scholastic Press, a division of Scholastic Inc.
SCHOLASTIC PRESS and colophon are trademarks of Scholastic Inc.

For information regarding permissions, write to Scholastic Inc.,
Attention: Permissions Department, 555 Broadway,
New York, NY 10012.

Library of Congress Cataloging-in-Publication Data Available

ISBN 0-590-02911-8

10 9 8 7 6 5 0/0 01 02 03
Printed in Mexico 49 First edition, September 1998

Bunny Reads Back

Your child's first board books by Rosemary Wells

What are Bunny Reads Back books? Familiar children's songs in board book format that will get your preschoolers turning pages, looking at pictures, and memorizing words. Soon they'll be "reading" back to you!

ISBN 0-590-02911-8

50495

EAN

9 780590 029117

$4.95 US / $6.99 CAN

SCHOLASTIC